The Marriage Gift

Stephen Evans

For fun.

This is a work of fiction. The names, characters, places, and incidents are either the products of the author's imagination or are used fictitiously, and any resemblance to actual persons living or dead, business establishments, events, or locales is entirely coincidental.

The Marriage Gift/ Stephen Evans/ Second Edition.

ISBN: 978-1-953725-40-0

Contents

"A good marriage is not a democracy. It is a series of contiguous tyrannies by mutual consent."

—Ralph Wilson

The Marriage of True Minds

PROLOGUE

Iris and Frank were sitting naked in her kitchen waiting for a bagel to toast, when he said:

"No one outside a marriage can know what happens inside. And no one inside can know either. But this is how I imagine it."

THE INVITATION

The first recorded wedding gift was the apple given to Eve by the serpent in the Garden of Eden. Unfortunately, the serpent made an unforgivable faux pas: the Knowledge of Good and Evil was not returnable.

www.Factuosity.com

At the coat closet, they silently perform a complicated ritual of grocery exchange, removing their jackets without putting down any of the bags. Once the jackets are off, the bags are redistributed with a coordination at once effortless and thoughtless.

James walks through the kitchen door first and holds the swinging door open as Paula enters. Then he lets it swing closed, stopping it with his foot without looking behind him.

They stand in front of their predestined locations (James at the refrigerator and Paula at the pantry) and begin to put the groceries away. When they come across an item that does not belong in their respective domains, they execute an automatic exchange, tossing the item to the other, condiments under air traffic control. Once the process is complete, the reusable cloth bags are folded and properly stored until the next shopping venture. Then they sit in their assigned seats at the kitchen table.

PAULA

Hungry?

James nods.

The ritual begins again, except in reverse, as they coordinate the construction of two sets of sandwiches. Only the drinks differ:

Milk for James.

Diet Coke for Paula.

There is still hope.

*　　*　　*

James is lying on the couch, watching a movie dubbed in Spanish.

Hola Butch.

Hola Sundance.

Paula sits at the kitchen table, reviewing and sorting a stack of mail. She is armed with a sterling silver letter opener with a handle cast in the image of a snake swallowing its tail, probably a wedding gift, since no one would ever buy one like that for themselves.

Paula rips open an envelope, shredding the paper with the dull not quite tarnished but slightly discolored blade, then dumps the envelope in the trash can next to her. She fans out a stack of coupons like a deck of cards, then chooses one.

> PAULA
> Here's a coupon from that place.

She waves the coupon in the air like a flag of truce.

James doesn't move.

> JAMES
> I thought we didn't like that place.

> PAULA
> No, that's that other place. This is the place that had that good...

> JAMES
> Oh, that place. That had those little...

> PAULA
> Right. Anyway, I'm putting it in the coupon drawer.

Paula sets it in one of several piles of coupons.

James emits his trademark snortlaugh.

                    JAMES
     Future generations will thank you.

Paula turns, lifting an eyebrow. After all, it is James who insists on letting his life choices be driven by random postal discounts.

                    PAULA
     What does that mean?

James sighs, but manages to elevate off the couch. He crosses to the coupon drawer and pulls out two handfuls of old coupons.

                    JAMES
     In ten million years, an alien
     archaeologist is going to open this
     drawer and find coupon fossils. It will
     conclude that we foraged on these
     during the winter.

He is suddenly curious.

He tastes one.

It's not bad.

                    PAULA
     What do you suggest?

He grabs the latest coupon from the pile.

JAMES
I suggest we use it now. I'm still
hungry.

James goes to the phone and attempts to dial while holding the coupon three inches from his face. He succeeds, having had much practice because he can't find any of the twelve pairs of reading glasses he has placed carefully throughout the apartment.

Paula slices open another envelope, surgically extracts another coupon, and slides another envelope into the trash.

PAULA
Hey look, we either won a new
Cadillac, a microwave oven, or a
genuine cubic zirconium ring.

JAMES
Oh, I hope it's the ring.

James is nodding his head to the synthetic on-hold rhythm. He is shocked into awareness by a voice.

JAMES
Yes hum uh hum we'd like to order yes
I can hold.

Paula deposits the coupon in an alternate yet carefully chosen pile.

PAULA
Do you think all zirconium is cubic?

JAMES
I mean, where would we park it?

PAULA
The ring?

JAMES
No, the yes we'd like to order
555-2424.

Paula rips another envelope.

PAULA
Couldn't there be triangular zirconium?

Paula examines the phone bill.

JAMES
Wilson, yes. How'd you know that?

He covers the phone and whispers to Paula.

JAMES
How'd they know that?

Paula places the phone bill in the bill pile. The envelope flutters down into the trash.

PAULA
Octagonal zirconium?

JAMES
Yes, we'd like to order one of those
good...

She opens another one.

PAULA
Dodecahedral zirconium.

JAMES
You knew that too?

He covers the phone again.

JAMES
I think I called the Psychic Pizza
Network.

He uncovers the phone.

PAULA
And make sure it has lots of those
little...

She tears the envelope in half and releases it
into the trash.

PAULA
You're not listening to me.

JAMES
I'm experiencing the miracle of
modern technology.

PAULA
Tesseractal zirconium.

JAMES
How long?

PAULA
When eternity just isn't enough.

JAMES
That's a long time.

She tears the picture up and tosses it in the trash.

PAULA
It is with someone who doesn't listen.

JAMES
No it's fine. Thank you.

He hangs up.

JAMES
I could make it myself in less time than that.

She rips opens another envelope.

PAULA
But then it wouldn't have those little...

The envelope flutters into the trash.

JAMES
True.

She holds up a square ecru card and reads the engraved invitation.

PAULA
Hey, we're invited to a wedding.

JAMES
What were you saying?

Paula reads.

PAULA
Hope you can come, Cousin Angela.

James collapses back onto the couch.

JAMES
Something about the circus?

PAULA
It's on Saturday.

He flips the channel.

JAMES
Or Octopuses?

Another channel.

PAULA
That's three days.

Another channel.

JAMES
Octopuses in the circus?

PAULA
You'll have to get a gift.

She tosses the invitation to James. The stiff card helicopters through the air towards James in a swift parabolic motion. He flails, trying to catch it, misses, picks it up off the floor.

> JAMES
> What's this?

He reads.

> JAMES
> Hope you can come, Cousin Angela.

Paula picks up another envelope, tears it open, trashes the envelope.

> PAULA
> The wedding is Saturday, so you need
> to get the gift right away.

James nods.

> JAMES
> Okay.

Paula smiles and waits.

> JAMES
> Wait. What? Time out.

Paula sorts through the minutiae of the cable bill.

> PAULA
> You could get her an octopus.

JAMES
I need to get the gift?

She puts it in the bill pile.

PAULA
Or tickets to the circus.

He reads the invitation again.

JAMES
Why do I need to get the gift?

Paula turns to him.

PAULA
She's your cousin.

JAMES
She is?

PAULA
Well, she's not my cousin.

James examines the invitation carefully. Forgotten knowledge, lost for ten long and busy years, floods his brain. James old life flashes in front of him, at the end of which he became for a brief and not altogether happy time an initiate in the mysteries of ecru.

JAMES
I don't remember any Cousin Angela.

PAULA
There are two possibilities: she's your
cousin or she's my cousin. Which
means I forgot her or you forgot her.
Which do you think is more likely?

James goes to the closet and gets his jacket.

JAMES
Save me some pizza.

PAULA
Where are you going?

JAMES
I'm going to see my parents. If she's my
cousin, they'll know.

Paula shrugs, doubting the logic but knowing
the futility of meddling in James' family
matters.

PAULA
Hurry back.

James rushes out the door. Paula mutters after
the door slams.

PAULA
I make no pizza guarantees.

*   *   *

In the hallway, the Bartlett's are leaving their apartment across the hall.

James nods pleasantly.

They nod pleasantly back.

> JAMES
>
> After you

He sweeps his hand down the hall toward the elevator.

> MRS. BARTLETT
>
> Thank you.

They walk down the hall to the elevator. James arrives behind them, and presses the Down button.

They wait.

After a moment, Mr. Bartlett presses it after him.

They wait.

> JAMES
>
> Does that work?

> MR. BARTLETT
>
> Excuse me?

> JAMES
>
> I've always wondered. The elevator doesn't come so you press the button again. Does that work?

> MRS. BARTLETT
>
> I have no idea.

They wait some more.

Mr. Bartlett presses the button again.

> JAMES
>
> So if you don't know whether it works, why do you do it?

> MRS. BARTLETT
>
> It's better than nothing.

James shrugs.

> JAMES
>
> Good point.

They wait some more.

> JAMES
>
> But is it really?

> MRS. BARTLETT
>
> Excuse me?

> JAMES

Is it really better to push a button even though you have no idea whether it will help? What if it hurts? What if it delays the elevator? What if it just gets more and more confused and tired of having the same button pushed over and over again. Maybe the elevator is fine as it is. Maybe the elevator should be allowed to continue instead of being constantly interrupted. Maybe we should just let the elevator go on and on and on and on...

The Bartletts move as far away from James as possible.

> JAMES

What if the elevator forgets why it is moving in the first place. That would not be good. In fact, that would be bad. Very very bad!

The elevator door opens.

> JAMES

After you.

The Bartletts get in, eyeing James with alarm. Mr. Bartlett places his arm around his wife.

James smiles.

> JAMES
I'll take the next one.

The door closes.

*   *   *

The living room hasn't changed since 1973, except for the addition of an enormous flat screen television balanced precariously on a tiny faux brass metal stand. Thin plastic wheels drive deep into the once plush carpet.

Pop is sitting in a recliner in his undershirt and shorts.

> JAMES
I'm here.

> POP
Strike up the band.

James flops down on the couch, mooches some of Pop's popcorn.

> JAMES
Nice, Pop.

> POP
That's what I'm watching. Judy Garland and Mickey Rooney.

James nods.

> POP
> What a lovely girl. Such a shame.

> JAMES
> Judy Garland?

> POP
> Mickey Rooney was married eight
> times.

> JAMES
> Really.

> POP
> That's persistence.

> JAMES
> True.

They watch in silence for a moment.

> JAMES
> Where's Ma?

> POP
> Where else?

Pop starts singing *Strike Up the Band*. James goes into the Kitchen. Ma is making cookies.

> JAMES
> I'm here.

> MA
> Strike up the band.

JAMES
Yeah, I saw.

MA
Saw what?

She wipes some flour from her cheek and leans toward James for a kiss.

JAMES
Never mind.

He kisses her cheek.

MA
Have a cookie.

James sits at the table.

JAMES
Ma, who is Cousin Angela?

MA
Never heard of her. Have a cookie.

James has a cookie.

MA
Oatmeal cranberry. They were out of raisins at the grocery store. Who ever heard of a grocery store being out of raisins? Or maybe they moved them. They're always moving the raisins. Maybe they're fruit. Maybe they're

candy. Someone should talk to the
manager.

JAMES
She must be a relative of ours. Paula
and I were invited to her wedding and
Paula's never heard of her.

MA
Harold?

Pop replies without stirring.

POP
What? I'm watching Judy.

Ma wipes the flour from her hands.

MA
We weren't invited to your niece's
wedding.

JAMES
No, Ma, I'm not even sure—

POP
I can't hear you. I'm watching Judy.

Though she is a tiny woman, Ma fills the
doorway between the kitchen and the living
room. There is no way around her.

MA
Call your brother. Your niece Angela is getting married and we weren't invited.

JAMES
You know, Ma, it's possible—

POP
I don't have a niece named Angela. My niece is named Sarah. Your niece is named Angela. Call your sister and find out why we weren't invited.

JAMES
I really don't even want to go—

Ma goes back to making cookies.

MA
He doesn't know.

POP
I'm watching Judy.

She starts pounding the cookie dough.

MA
If they don't want us, we won't go.

JAMES
So, Ma. Who is Cousin Angela?

MA
Never heard of her. Have a cookie.

James takes another cookie.

                    JAMES
Bye, Ma.

                    MA
Strike up the band.

                    JAMES
What?

                    MA
Your father is watching Judy.

He kisses her cheek again and leaves.

*   *   *

James and the Bartletts are riding up in the elevator.

Silent tension prevails.

The door opens on their floor.

                    JAMES
After you.

They rush past.

James lets them reach their door before he exits the elevator.

*　　*　　*

Paula is on the couch with S.C.U.B.A, the spaniel-husky mix adopted from the local shelter six years before whose ears hint at extraterrestrial origin. She (Paula) is eating pizza and watching television. James dives for the box (of pizza).

PAULA
You should call your father. Judy is on.

JAMES
Strike up the Band.

PAULA
Meet Me in St. Louis.

James sits next to her on the couch.

PAULA
So. Who is Cousin Angela?

JAMES
There is no Cousin Angela.

They watch for a while. Judy is singing *The Boy Next Door*. Paula revolves her legs over James' lap, briefly disturbing S.C.U.B.A.'s pizza reverie.

PAULA
Then why is she getting married?

JAMES
I'll be sure and ask as soon as I create
her out of thin air.

They munch for a minute.

PAULA
Hey, check the guestbook.

JAMES
Great idea.

He gets up, looks around.

JAMES
What guestbook?

PAULA
Ours. Maybe she came to our wedding.

JAMES
Great idea.

He doesn't move.

JAMES
Where is it?

PAULA
I guess with the other wedding stuff.

James goes into the bedroom: neat, warm, comfortable. Pillows and candles and stuff. He starts taking things out of the closet.

Extra pillows.

Sheets.

An old racquet ball.

Candles.

Unidentified stuff.

> PAULA
> Under the bed!

James pushes everything back into the closet and crawls over the queen bed and pulls out a box from underneath. He can barely breathe through the cloud of dust that rises.

He finds the guestbook and flips through, able to read about a third of the names, recognizing about half of those. No Angela.

He opens an album of photographs. Page after page of happy wedding shots. Photos of the honeymoon in Maui.

Sailing.

Parasailing.

Scuba diving.

Cliff diving (watching).

Paula is wearing a red bikini. James is wearing matching bright red swim trunks.

He closes the book, stuffs everything back into the box, and shoves it under the bed. He walks back out into the living room and sits on the couch. Paula returns her legs to his lap. Judy is dancing with her grandfather.

JAMES
No Cousin Angela.

PAULA
Ask your brother.

JAMES
Frank? Why?

PAULA
He probably knows her.

JAMES
He probably does. In the biblical sense.

PAULA
Ewwww.

Paula punches him on the shoulder.

JAMES
I'm kidding.

PAULA
Ewwww.

She punches him again.

JAMES
Try living with him.

> PAULA

Ewwww.

He jumps up, throwing her legs into the pizza box, thereby spinning it onto the floor, drawing the immediate attention of S.C.U.B.A.

> JAMES

S.C.U.B.A.! No processed foods.

Paula picks up the box and claims another piece of pizza.

> PAULA

Just go.

> JAMES

Ewwww.

He puts his sweatshirt back on and opens the front door, peeking both ways out of the door.

Paula mumbles through the mushrooms.

> PAULA

Wah-ah-oo-ooing?

James speaks fluent pizza.

> JAMES
> Looking to see if there's a clear path to the elevator.

Paula swallows.

PAULA

Why?

JAMES

The neighbors. Across the way.

Paula goes to the door and peers out too.

PAULA

The Bartletts?

James nods.

JAMES

They are a little weird.

PAULA

I was thinking of inviting them over for
dinner next week.

James peeks out again, then whispers.

JAMES

The guy has a button fetish.

PAULA

Ewww.

James pulls away reflexively, expecting a
punch. Paula looks out warily.

PAULA

How do you know?

JAMES

Long story.

He kisses her quickly.

> JAMES
> It's safe. I'm off.

He dashes down the hall. Paula closes the door.

> PAULA
> Some people should not live in the city.

*　　*　　*

At the elevator, James pushes the button once.

He almost pushes it again, but decides against it.

But he can't help himself.

He pushes it again.

Then again and again.

The elevator arrives and he gets in.

The door closes.

Down the hall, Mr. Bartlett peeks out of his door.

> MR. BARTLETT
> It's safe.

*   *   *

Frank is waiting in a booth at the back of the bar. A baseball hat is pulled down low over his eyes.

James enters, looks around, and finally spots Frank in the back. He navigates through the heavy wooden tables spread out across the blank wooden floor. On each table, the peanuts in the bowl have fused into strangely familiar shapes. A car. A circus. An octopus. James slides into the booth opposite Frank.

JAMES
Why are you hiding back here?

Frank glances out from under the bill of his baseball cap.

FRANK
I think I was thrown out of this bar
once.

James peers around, casing the joint for danger.

JAMES
Then why did you want to meet here?

Frank shrugs.

> FRANK
> It's a nice place.

James nods. It is a nice place. If you have a tattoo you can't show anyone.

> JAMES
> Why were you thrown out?

Frank shrugs.

> FRANK
> It's a nice place.

A waitress passes by, colorfully dressed.

> JAMES
> Can we get a couple of beers?

The waitress looks suspiciously at Frank.

> WAITRESS
> Frank?

> FRANK
> Oh hi!

Frank whispers to James.

> FRANK
> It's coming back to me.

The waitress raises an eyebrow then leaves to get the drinks.

> FRANK
> So, what's up?

                    JAMES
Did you get invited to Cousin Angela's
wedding?

                    FRANK
Cousin who?

                    JAMES
Angela.

                    FRANK
No. Did you?

James pulls out the invitation and hands it to
Frank, who examines it front and back.

                    FRANK
That's strange.

                    JAMES
Why?

Frank waves at the waitress. The bartender
gives Frank a mean look.

                    FRANK
She never liked you.

                    JAMES
You remember her?

                    FRANK
No.

> JAMES
Then how do you know she never liked
me?

Frank hands the invitation back to James.

> FRANK
Because there is no Cousin Angela.

James takes the invitation and stuffs it in his
pocket.

> JAMES
I see.

> FRANK
Plus, none of our cousins liked you.

> JAMES
That's not true.

The waitress brings the beer.

> FRANK
They thought you were a snob.

James leans forward.

> JAMES
Me?

> FRANK
I'm just saying.

James sits back in the booth.

JAMES
I'm not a snob.

The waitress and Frank begin to flirt silently. The bartender gives them both a mean look.

FRANK
Absolutely not, I agree. You're just—

Frank makes a vague figure with his hands.

JAMES
What?

Frank shrugs.

FRANK
Pretentious.

JAMES
No way!

FRANK
Elitist?

Frank nods to the waitress.

JAMES
I am not.

Frank shrugs and winks at the waitress. She laughs, until the bartender looms ominously behind her.

BARTENDER
Is there a problem here?

The waitress points to James.

>
> WAITRESS
> He's a pretentious elitist snob.

She laughs again.

The bartender grabs James.

>
> BARTENDER
> Okay, you're out of here!

Frank stands.

>
> FRANK
> Hey, leave my brother alone.

The bartender grabs Frank too.

>
> BARTENDER
> Okay. You're both out of here.

The bartender escorts them out. Roughly.

The waitress yells after them.

>
> WAITRESS
> Call me! I mean the cute one. Not the
> pretentious elitist snob.

* * *

The bartender shoves James and Frank out of
the door. They adjust their clothes, sit on the

curb under a streetlight. It has just rained, so the night is slick and glimmery, and wet.

> JAMES
> So how did you get thrown out last time?

> FRANK
> It's coming back to me.

James shakes his head.

> JAMES
> This only happens to me when I'm with you.

Frank puts his arm around James' shoulder.

> FRANK
> You're welcome.

James shakes him off.

> JAMES
> So. You're saying you don't know Cousin Angela?

> FRANK
> No. I'm saying there is no Cousin Angela. Not in our family anyway.

There is a 29 second pause.

> JAMES
> Maybe it's an alias.

Frank nods.

> FRANK
> Using an alias to get married. Clever.

> JAMES
> What have you got against marriage?

> FRANK
> For mythical cousins, not a thing.

A cab drives by and splashes them.

> FRANK
> My point exactly.

James and Frank get up and amble along the darkened street, walking, striding, and jumping in elaborate patterns to avoid the puddles on the sidewalk. James stops.

> JAMES
> What _do_ you think of marriage?

Frank throws him a concerned look.

> FRANK
> Why?

> JAMES
> Just wondering.

A car races by.

> FRANK
> You and Paula okay?

> JAMES

Yeah. We're good. Amazing.

Another car races down the street, chasing the first car. Apparently. Never assume.

> FRANK

So?

James shrugs.

> FRANK

Yeah.

A police car zooms by, sirens blaring. Chasing. Apparently.

They walk in silence for a few moments.

> FRANK

Men don't fall in love. They blink into it. And whatever they see after the blink is what they love. And what they see then never changes in their eyes. Because once you're in love you can't blink anymore. That's what love is: eternal unblinkableness.

> JAMES

Apparently.

They stop at James' car.

> JAMES

You want a lift?

An ambulance goes screaming by.

FRANK
No. I think I knew that waitress.

*   *   *

Paula is in bed, reading. James walks in soaking wet.

PAULA
Is it raining?

JAMES
Depends on where you're sitting.

He starts to undress.

PAULA
So?

JAMES
What?

PAULA
Who is Cousin Angela?

JAMES
There is no Cousin Angela.

Paula sits on the bed.

PAULA
Then why is she getting married?

JAMES
Presumably for the same reason
anyone gets married.

Paula closes her book.

PAULA
When did this become my fault?

JAMES
When you opened the invitation.

Paula slides into bed.

PAULA
So we won't go.

JAMES
Of course we won't go. There is no
Cousin Angela.

PAULA
So fine.

JAMES
Good.

James fluffs the pillow. Hard.

JAMES
All I'm saying is.

PAULA
I'm agreeing with you.

James wrestles the pillow to the mattress and lies down.

JAMES
But what kind of agreement?

PAULA
What are you asking me?

James rolls over, facing her.

JAMES
Are you agreeing because you think I'm right?

Paula rolls to face him.

PAULA
Yes.

She rolls away.

JAMES
Or are you agreeing because you don't want to go to the wedding anyway?

PAULA
No. I want to go to the wedding.

JAMES
I knew it!

She rolls back to him.

PAULA
But there is no wedding.

James rolls away, and stares at the ceiling.

> JAMES
> So what you are saying is that you agree with me but secretly plan to punish me because you want to go to the wedding and I don't.

Paula gets out of bed.

> PAULA
> You don't?

> JAMES
> No. There is no wedding.

> PAULA
> But that's not why.

James gets out of bed.

> JAMES
> There is no Cousin Angela.

> PAULA
> Why don't you want to go to the wedding?

> JAMES
> Fine. I do want to go.

They both get back in bed.

> PAULA
> Then we'll go.

JAMES
Fine.

James turns out the lights.

PAULA
You'll have to get a gift.

James sighs.

THE CHOICE

Ice crushers are the fourth most popular wedding gift in Minnesota, after toasters, coffee makers, and silver-plated Lutefisk tongs.

www.Factuosity.com

Paula and Iris are eating lunch in the kitchen at work.

> IRIS
>
> No. You are absolutely right.

> PAULA
>
> Really?

> IRIS
>
> I'm pretty sure.

> PAULA
>
> Really?

> IRIS
>
> It's free food and beer. No man turns down free food and beer. It's genetic.

Paula puts down her sandwich and gets up to pour herself a cup of coffee.

> PAULA
That sounds right.

> IRIS
I'm pretty sure.

Paula sits back down.

> PAULA
But why?

> IRIS
It's an unconscious impulse.

Paula takes a sip of her coffee. She doesn't notice the coffee is terrible. She takes another sip and shakes her head.

> PAULA
I don't think James has any unconscious impulses.

Iris shakes her head.

> IRIS
Men are more complicated than we think.

> PAULA
You think?

Iris nods, mouth full.

> PAULA
So I should worry?

Iris shrugs, still chewing.

                    PAULA
But if he buys the gift, doesn't that
mean he doesn't have any unconscious
impulses?

                    IRIS
Yes, but only when he's conscious.

Paula nods.

                    PAULA
I can live with that.

*   *   *

James and Paula are sitting at the kitchen table, having dinner and reading the newspaper. S.C.U.B.A is by his water bowl, eyes glittering.

                    JAMES
Why me?

                    PAULA
Why you what?

James lowers his paper shield.

                    JAMES
Why do I have to get the gift?

Paula lowers hers too.

PAULA
She's your cousin.

JAMES
Ah. There. No. She's not.

Paula lifts an eyebrow, tilts her head, and leans in, knowing she will enjoy the strangled rationalization that is sure to follow.

JAMES
But, even if, hypothetically, she is my cousin, does it necessarily follow that I have to buy the gift?

James pauses. It's coming.

JAMES
I think.

It's coming.

JAMES
The spouse

Almost there.

JAMES
That has the most.

Ahhhh.

JAMES
Refined sense of taste and the greatest understanding of the needs of a newly

married person this argument isn't working, is it?

Paula waits.

PAULA
Fine.

She raises the paper up again.

JAMES
What's fine?

PAULA
I'll buy the gift. It's no problem.

JAMES
Good.

James raises his paper up again.

Paula corrects him.

PAULA
No. It's not good. It's fine.

JAMES
Good. It's good that it's fine.

Paula lowers her paper. She glances around the kitchen and wonders what it will be like to live in this space alone.

PAULA
Fine.

James drops his paper.

> JAMES

What did I do?

Paula raises her paper again.

> PAULA

You have impulses.

> JAMES

What?

> PAULA

You have impulses. I didn't believe it.
But you do.

> JAMES

I suppose. On occasion.

> PAULA

Fine. Enjoy them. See if I care.

> JAMES

I don't understand.

> PAULA

Obviously.

> JAMES

Fine.

He puts his paper up again. She pulls it down
and takes his hand.

> PAULA

You're my husband. I have complete
confidence in you.

James nods.

> JAMES
> Fine. Good. No problem. I can do it.

*   *   *

> JAMES
> I can't do it.

James and Frank are standing in line at Taco Heaven.

> FRANK
> No way.

> JAMES
> I mean.

> FRANK
> Exactly. It's genetic. This is not just going to the store.

They move up one step in line.

> FRANK
> This means venturing into areas where men are programmed by nature not to go.

> JAMES
> Such as?

The Man In Line Behind them interrupts.

                    M.I.L.B.
The china department.

                    JAMES
Ewwww.

The Man In Line Ahead of them chimes in.

                    M.I.L.A.
The crystal department.

Frank and James shudder.

                    FRANK
The bridal registry alone could land
you in therapy for years.

The man ahead and man behind concur.

                    JAMES
You're right.

They move up one step.

                    JAMES
Are you happy?

The Man In Line Behind steps in to answer.

James stops him.

                    JAMES
Let's let him take this one.

The Man In Line Ahead and the Man In Line Behind nod and turn away.

Frank pauses as if perusing the menu but in fact mentally examining his life history from the age of 13 on.

> FRANK
> Happiness is an alien concept.

> JAMES
> What does that mean?

Frank looks around to make sure no one can hear.

> FRANK
> Do you know the origin of the word happiness?

James shrugs.

> JAMES
> No.

They move up one step.

> FRANK
> Neither does anyone else. There is no record of the word 'happiness' in any human language before 1947.

> JAMES
> What happened in 1947?

FRANK
Only a little event in Roswell, New
Mexico.

They move up one step.

James pauses as if perusing the menu but in fact mentally examining Frank's medical history from the age of 13 on.

JAMES
So you think happiness is an alien plot?

Frank shakes his head, not back and forth so much as an infinity sign, which any alien would recognize.

FRANK
Not a plot. More like, misery loves
company.

James nods, mentally speculating on Frank's medical history for the next few years.

JAMES
Ah.

They move up one step.

*   *   *

James and Frank are sitting at a table at Taco Heaven. Frank's SuperSpecialTacoDelight is so big he can barely get two hands around it.

> FRANK
> Are you happy?

James hesitates.

> JAMES
> My marriage is the best thing that ever happened to me.

> FRANK
> But?

> JAMES
> It keeps happening.

> FRANK
> You don't mean that.

Frank holds the taco over his open mouth and lets the contents drip in slowly.

> JAMES
> I know that. You think I think I don't know what I mean when I say what I think?

Frank chews for several minutes before saying:

> FRANK
> Yes. Starting with that sentence.

JAMES
If I ever lost Paula, I don't think I could
live with myself.

Frank gently lays his hand on James' shoulder.

FRANK
Well you can't live with me.

James shakes Frank off, nearly causing a salsa
incident.

JAMES
You're right.

Frank smiles wide and turns the taco sideways.
Somehow it fits.

James takes a deep breath.

JAMES
I am married to the woman I was
always meant to love, and I miss her
every minute I am away from her.

FRANK
Your secret is safe with me.

JAMES
My life is everything I ever hoped it
could be.

FRANK
Then you know what you should do?

> JAMES

What?

> FRANK

Shut up and eat.

James nods and smiles wide.

> JAMES

Good tip.

They munch in silence for a while. Except for the munching.

> JAMES

You should get married again.

Frank shakes his head, dislodging a bit of guacamole from his chin.

> FRANK

All the good ones are...

James waits a few moments.

> JAMES

Are what?

> FRANK

Good.

> JAMES

I see.

Frank puts down the taco remnants and gazes eagerly at James' fries.

FRANK
Are you going to finish those fries?

James examines the fries closely.

JAMES
I haven't started them yet.

FRANK
It's still a valid question.

James shrugs.

JAMES
Fine.

He pushes the fries over to Frank.

*   *   *

Paula and Iris are sitting in a conference room at work. Someone at the head of the table is speaking, but no one seems to be listening, including Paula and Iris.

PAULA
He's going to do it.

IRIS
What?

PAULA
The gift. He's going to buy it.

IRIS
Oh. That's a relief.

PAULA
You're telling me.

They pay attention for a bit to the droning voice.

IRIS
Unless...

PAULA
What?

Iris begins to draw mystical symbols on the conference report in front of her.

IRIS
Unless this is a ploy.

Paula shakes her head.

PAULA
I don't think so.

They pay attention again.

PAULA
What kind of ploy?

Iris begins to diagram the situation over the non-profit projection.

IRIS
He can't just refuse. It is his cousin.

> PAULA
> Actually, she doesn't exist.

Iris puts dotted lines around the figure of the cousin.

> IRIS
> So he'll try some other way. Play on your sympathy.

> PAULA
> I don't think so.

They pay attention again.

> PAULA
> You think?

> IRIS
> Wait and see.

*   *   *

James and Paula are sitting together on the couch watching TV, an old black and white movie. Something with Rosalind Russell.

Paula is waiting to see if James is going to bring it up.

James isn't sure how to bring it up.

They both say nothing.

*   *   *

The light is off in the bedroom. Neither one is asleep. After a few silent moments:

PAULA

What?

JAMES

I didn't say anything.

PAULA

Of course not.

James turns to her.

JAMES

I have nothing to say.

He turns back. There is quiet for a few more moments.

PAULA

I know you want to say it.

James turns to her.

JAMES

Believe me. I don't.

He turns back. There is quiet for a few more moments.

James sighs.

>   JAMES
> I was thinking maybe a toaster.

>   PAULA
> Fine.

*   *   *

Paula and Iris are drinking 'coffee' in the office kitchen.

>   PAULA
> We're giving them a toaster.

Iris spins away, spilling her vanilla mint cappuccino.

>   PAULA
> What?

Iris turns back, tears in her eyes, unable to speak.

>   PAULA
> What is it?

Iris breathes deeply, shakes her head, then breathes deeply again.

>   IRIS
> I'm sorry. It's just that I've often
> thought that if Stan and I had had the

right toaster, our marriage might have
been saved.

Paula moves closer.

PAULA
What makes you think that?

Iris wipes her eyes.

IRIS
Stan used to get up in the middle of the
night and make toast. The toaster we
had would leave crumbs on the counter
and he would never clean them up. So
every morning for seven years, I would
get up and clean up the crumbs on the
counter. And every morning I would
complain about the crumbs, and we'd
start to fight and finally he left.

Paula sighs.

PAULA
Did he take the toaster?

Iris shakes her head.

IRIS
I gave it away. Too many memories.

Paula sits back. She entwines her middle finger
around a cheese doodle. Tiny doodle grains
fall to her palm, forming images on her hand,

pictographs in an incomprehensible junk food idiom.

Possibly a ring.

Or a circus.

Or an octopus.

She gazes at the inscrutable figures, wondering at their meaning. Doodle grains. Toast crumbs. There is a significance, a serendipitous collusion of metaphor, that she can't quite grasp. She knows a marriage depends on it. But whose?

> PAULA
> We gave you that toaster, didn't we?

Iris rallies, and comforts Paula.

> IRIS
> I don't blame you. If it hadn't been the toaster, it would have been some other appliance.

Paula and Iris hug. The other employees in the kitchen leave silently and quickly.

> PAULA
> I'm so sorry. We didn't know.

> IRIS
> Neither did we. Neither did we.

*   *   *

As Paula enters the apartment, James greets her with a wrapped gift in his hand.

JAMES
I bought the toaster.

PAULA
Take it back.

James drops the package.

JAMES
Excuse me?

PAULA
Take it back.

JAMES
I don't understand.

PAULA
You have to take it back.

James picks up the package and holds it out.

JAMES
But.

He looks at the package from several vantage points, unable to determine what could be wrong.

                    JAMES
I bought it. The wedding gift. I bought
it. That's what you wanted.

Paula is unmoved.

                    PAULA
It can't be a toaster.

James again holds out the package.

                    JAMES
But.

Paula shakes her head.

                    JAMES
Why not?

Paula turns away.

                    PAULA
I can't have that on my conscience
again.

James nods.

                    JAMES
Ohhhh.

Then.

                    JAMES
What?

Paula purses her lips.

                    PAULA
    Never again.

James shakes the package.

                    JAMES
    I think it's broken.

Paula nods.

                    PAULA
    Then we're safe.

*   *   *

James and Paula are having breakfast and reading the paper. James is flipping through Section C, looking at advertisements.

                    JAMES
    There are too many choices.

                    PAULA
    For what?

                    JAMES
    For the wedding gift. There's no way to narrow it down.

Paula puts down Section A and picks up Section D.

PAULA
Look at it this way. If Cousin Angela
doesn't exist, then she must need
everything.

James puts down Section C and picks up
Section A.

JAMES
I don't think I can buy her reality.

Paula folds Section D carefully, so as not to
crease the article on day spas. The idea of a
day spa is becoming more and more attractive
to her, compelling almost, like a Madeleine
with her tea in the morning, if she drank tea.
But she doesn't know why. She has historically
avoided day spas, though other kinds of spas
did not seem to elicit the same deep emotional
revulsion. Perhaps the article can provide
some answers. There is a significance, a
serendipitous collusion of underlying
metaphor, that she can't quite grasp. She
knows a marriage depends on it. But whose?

PAULA
You are making this way too difficult.
Just think back to when we were first
married. What did we need?

JAMES
Sex.

PAULA
Too difficult to wrap.

Paula puts down Section D and picks up Section E. James puts down Section A, picks up Section D, and wonders whether day spas offer gift certificates.

JAMES
What about a sex toy of some kind?

PAULA
They're newlyweds. They are sex toys.

JAMES
I wonder where they're going on their honeymoon.

PAULA
They're newlyweds. It doesn't matter.

Paula puts down Section E of the paper and picks up Section F. James puts down Section D and picks up Section E.

JAMES
You're not being very helpful.

Paula puts down Section F. James puts down Section E and tries to pick up Section F, but Paula puts her hand on his.

PAULA
You don't remember, do you?

                    JAMES
What?

                    PAULA
What it was like when we were first
married.

                    JAMES
I remember.

Paula's eyebrows levitate.

                    JAMES
It was great.

Paula sighs.

                    PAULA
You don't remember what it was like to
wake up in the morning and be so
grateful to see you there. You don't
remember how it was physically
painful to not be touching you. You
don't remember how thrilling it was
when we stopped saying yours and
mine and started saying ours.

James nods.

                    JAMES
I remember. It was great.

Paula hands him Section F.

PAULA
It was. Wasn't it?

*   *   *

James and Frank are playing one on one. James is dribbling left and right. Frank doesn't move.

JAMES
She didn't like the toaster.

FRANK
Why?

James dribbles right. Frank doesn't move.

JAMES
It wasn't clear. I mean, it was clear that she didn't like it. But why wasn't clear.

FRANK
That's ridiculous. The toaster is the progenitor of civilized life. ·

James dribbles left. Frank doesn't move.

JAMES
And you're now going to tell me why.

Frank walks up to an adjacent brick wall covered with graffiti. James sits on the basketball and watches.

                    FRANK
When the cave men first made toast,
they held it too close to the fire and got
burnt greasy crumbs all over their
fingers and when they wiped them on
the wall of the cave it formed shapes
like the saber-toothed antelope and
suddenly Art was born.

James tosses Frank the ball.

                    JAMES
You tell me that story and I swear to
God I'm convinced you were there.

Frank bows.

                    FRANK
Thank you. Thank you.

                    JAMES
I got chills.

                    FRANK
E Pluribus Toastmaster.

                    JAMES
Caveat Emptor.

                    FRANK
Exactly.

                    JAMES
So what are we playing for?

FRANK
What d'you got?

James doesn't move as Frank drives past him.

*   *   *

Pop is sitting in his recliner in his undershirt and shorts. James walks in.

JAMES
Hey Pop.

POP
What's wrong?

James flops down in a chair.

JAMES
Nothing.

Pop turns toward the kitchen.

POP
Something's wrong with James!

Ma calls from the kitchen.

MA
Have a cookie!

James sighs.

              JAMES
There's nothing wrong.

Pop reaches down and pulls the handle on the recliner, thrusting himself forward and almost into the coffee table. He points his finger at James.

              POP
You don't come here in the middle of
the day because everything is all right.

James shrugs.

              JAMES
It's 8:30. I'm fine. I just have to buy a
wedding gift.

Pop re-reclines.

              POP
Every married man has to buy a
wedding gift at least once. It's a rite of
passage.

They watch in silence as Pop flips channels.

              JAMES
What are you looking for?

              POP
What d'you got?

Pop flips more channels.

James sighs.

JAMES
How do you keep it going after all
these years, Pop?

POP
We take turns forgetting things.

James nods.

POP
It keeps it lively.

James nods.

JAMES
I can imagine.

Pop flips more channels.

JAMES
Where's Ma?

POP
Where else?

Pop flips more channels.

*   *   *

In the kitchen, Ma is arranging flowers.

JAMES
Hi Ma.

                    MA
What's wrong?

James shrugs.

                    JAMES
Where did the flowers come from?

                    MA
Your father buys them for me every
day.

Ma breaks up in laughter.

                    MA
Sorry. I can't keep a straight face.

James nods.

                    JAMES
I have to buy a wedding gift.

Ma keeps arranging.

                    MA
Sit.

                    JAMES
No. I have to go.

                    MA
Sit.

James sits at the kitchen table.

                    MA
So?

James shrugs.

                JAMES
I was just wondering if you had any
ideas.

Ma viciously snips the bottoms off the stems.

                MA
I have ideas.

James waits.

                JAMES
So?

Ma takes a clear glass vase down from the shelf. It is shaped like her, like a woman, like some women, like a form ascribed to women since the days of the Neolithic fertility totems. James had studied these totems while filming a documentary about Salma Hayek, and it occurs to him that a vase might make an excellent wedding present. Who could object to a vase? It is beautiful and practical. And easy to find.

Ma fills the vase halfway with water from the tap, then drops in two Alka-Seltzer tablets, which start to dissolve immediately.

James wonders where this vase came from. Was it a wedding gift? He harkens back to his childhood days in St. Cloud, playing in the street as Ma worked in her garden. Had she then transported the products of that garden to that self-same vase? Did it represent his childhood feelings of security, or love, of a world that at the same time made sense and yet was full of wonder? Was that why he felt so strongly that a vase was the right, the proper, the only choice he could make?

No. Probably came from Target, the only store that Ma and Pop will both enter.

MA

So do you?

Ma adds two teaspoons of Tupelo honey to the vase.

James leans in, elbows on the table, hands supporting his chin, mesmerized by the sight of the honey sinking and the bubbles rising.

JAMES

Do I what?

Ma brushes his hair back from his face. It is a gesture arresting in its familiarity and history.

MA

Do you still love her?

James' eyes have not drifted from the vase.

     JAMES
What are you making?
Chrysanthemum-ade?

She swirls the liquid in the vase.

     MA
Show her.

     JAMES
With flowers?

Ma laughs again.

     MA
Have a cookie.

James takes a cookie.

    *   *   *

Mr. Bartlett and James are riding up the elevator. There is a long uncomfortable silence.

     JAMES
You're married, aren't you?

     MR. BARTLETT
Why do you ask?

     JAMES
Just making conversation.

Mr. Bartlett moves to the other side of the elevator.

> MR. BARTLETT
> In that case, yes. I am.

> JAMES
> Good for you.

> MR. BARTLETT
> Thank you.

There is another uncomfortable silence. Both of them eye the buttons suspiciously.

> MR. BARTLETT
> You've met my wife.

> JAMES
> Yes. You're a lucky man.

Bartlett leans on the panel, and his hand slips very close to the buttons. James watches intently.

> MR. BARTLETT
> Thank you. I am.

James takes a step toward the buttons.

> JAMES
> How long have you been married?

> MR. BARTLETT
> Twelve years.

James hand twitches, itching to regain button control.

> JAMES
> Ah. Ten for us.

> MR. BARTLETT
> Good on you.

> JAMES
> Ten wonderful years.

James moves his hand playfully over the buttons.

> JAMES
> Does your wife ever push your
> buttons?

> MR. BARTLETT
> Let's leave off the subject of buttons.

James nods.

> JAMES
> I understand. I mean, boy, do I
> understand. Actually, I don't
> understand. Do you understand?

The elevator stops and the door opens.

> MR. BARTLETT
> After you.

*　　*　　*

Paula is sitting on the couch, watching TV. James is at the desk looking through catalogues.

> JAMES
> I don't know what to get them.

Paula mutes.

> PAULA
> We shouldn't give them a wedding gift.

> JAMES
> We shouldn't?

> PAULA
> We should give them a Marriage Gift.

Paula stands. S.C.U.B.A comes to attention.

> PAULA
> We should give them a gift that will prepare them for the journey they are making together.

Paula turns to James.

> PAULA
> I mean think about it.

She puts a hand on each of his shoulders.

PAULA
These two people, who, let's face it,
barely knowing one another, at the
beginning of their adult lives, commit
to spending every day loving one
another, building their shared dreams,
pledging to care for and help and
inspire each other no matter what
happens or how either one of them
may change along the way.

She begins to shake James by the shoulders.

PAULA
We should give them a gift that
represents everything we believe about
marriage, a gift that will wish this
young couple all of the joy and laughter
and happiness we have had in our years
together.

James nods, a little dizzy.

JAMES
I'll try the mall.

Paula sits and unmutes.

PAULA
Whatever you think.

STEPHEN EVANS

The Quest

The Mall of America was originally constructed by the Mayan civilization after they migrated to Bloomington, Minnesota, in 832 AD. The edifice was quickly abandoned after the Mayans decided it was too damn cold and moved to a condo in Boca Raton. In the Mayan language, Boca Raton means "you are standing on my foot", which leads many archeologists to conclude that it was a two bedroom or possibly two bedroom with den. Oceanfront status is inconclusive and a subject of ongoing academic debate.

Mall of America lay empty for nearly four centuries, until Vikings discovered the abandoned shell in 1164 AD. The intrepid Norse explorers converted the building into a trading post for runes. Runes were bought and sold at the outpost for several generations, until the devastating Rune Bubble collapse of 1218, when many fortunes were lost. The phrase 'he was runed' entered common usage about this time.

The structure was once again abandoned until German and Swedish immigrants purchased the land in 1843 from the Lakota nation, who were trying to unload the building as a tax write-off. The immigrant community renovated the structure using plans developed by English philosopher Jeremy Bentham, and renamed it The Grand Panshoppeticon. This name proved too long for the shingles of the time and was later reduced to The Shoppe.

In the 1950s, the area was converted into a ballpark known as Metropolitan Stadium until a home run by slugger Harmon Killebrew triggered a massive earthquake on June 3, 1967. Finally in 1992, the facility was rebuilt in the shape of a dodecahedron and was renamed Mall of America, for unknown reasons.

The site has since become popular among American religious pilgrims for its health and spiritual benefits. A number of miracles are reported to have occurred on the grounds, including the Unlimited Credit Card Incident of 2003.

www.Factuosity.com

In the third-floor north food court of the Mall of America, James sits on the ledge of a large circular fountain. Spouts of water shoot out at odd angles from an abstract sculpture in the center. As shoppers are passing by, James tries to peek into their shopping bags. They don't appreciate it.

Frank walks up to James, stands watching silently, until James finally notices him.

> JAMES
> Thanks for coming.

Frank claps James on the back.

> FRANK
> Hey, what are brothers for? So. What
> are we doing here?

James curls his lower lip under his upper teeth.

> JAMES
> I have to buy a marriage gift.

Frank claps James on the back, harder this time.

> FRANK
> What are wives for? See ya.

James grabs his arm.

> JAMES
> I need you. I can't do this by myself.

Frank falls into the trap.

> FRANK
> What is a marriage gift anyway?

James tries to peek into a passing shopping bag, and gets smacked with the bag for his trouble.

> JAMES
> A marriage gift is a gift that if you don't buy exactly the right one your marriage falls apart.

> FRANK
> Ah. I see. Tricky. But why do you need me?

> JAMES
> Well. For starters, how do I know what people want when they're getting married?

> FRANK
> You're married.

James climbs up on the ledge of the fountain for better peeking vantage.

> JAMES
> That's exactly the point. I've already passed the marriage barrier. I can no longer imagine the illusions I held before entering into that state.

James leans over and drapes his arm around Frank's shoulder.

JAMES
You on the other hand are single and
harbor nothing but illusions about
marriage.

Frank shakes him off.

JAMES
So I think you are the most qualified to
judge what illusory people who are in
the process of becoming disillusioned
might want for a wedding gift.

Frank crosses his arms.

FRANK
You've been standing here this whole
time trying to come up with that pitiful
rationalization, haven't you?

JAMES
No. Not exactly. Yes.

Frank nods.

FRANK
But what you are really thinking is that
I'll think it's such a ridiculous excuse
that I'll feel sorry for you and stay and
help you.

James shrugs.

> JAMES
It crossed my mind.

Frank claps James on the back again. Really hard.

> FRANK
Well thought through.

> JAMES
Ow. I thought it might work. No one appreciates a good bad excuse more than you.

> FRANK
Thanks.

Frank considers pushing James into the fountain and making a run for it. But there are too many witnesses.

> JAMES
Where do we start?

James pulls Frank up onto the ledge of the fountain. A river of humanity passes beneath their purview, awe-inspiring in its commercial scope.

> JAMES
I've been watching these two stores.

James points to one store.

JAMES
I've noticed that people come out of
this store, but nobody ever goes in. I
think, maybe, there's some sort of
clone thing going on.

FRANK
Kind of a Jurassic Park for shoppers.

JAMES
Exactly. Follow me.

They trek perilously along the fountain ledge
to the opposite side. James points to another
store

JAMES
Now this store, on the other hand,
people go in, but no one comes out.

FRANK
So sort of a Twilight Zone, Soylent
Green kind of deal.

JAMES
Exactly.

They walk back around the ledge until they are
midway between the two stores.

JAMES
Now. I've considered the possibility
that there is a secret tunnel between
the two stores and that people go into

this store and come out that one. But I haven't been able to verify that yet.

FRANK
It's a promising theory.

JAMES
So the question is, which do we choose: The Twilight Zone or Jurassic Park?

FRANK
That's a tough one. Jurassic Park was classic Hollywood entertainment with a powerful social message. But The Twilight Zone was cool.

They stare at each other until James announces:

JAMES
An ordinary department store, teetering on the edge of...The Twilight Zone.

*   *   *

In the third-floor north food court of the Mall of America, Paula waits at a table, sipping a soda. In the background, a version of Puccini's Greatest Hits pierces the taco staccato.

Iris hurries in.

> PAULA
>
> Thanks for coming.

They hug.

> IRIS
>
> Hey, what are friends for?

> PAULA
>
> James is buying the wedding gift. I
> thought he might need backup.

Iris drops her purse in her excitement. A purple hairbrush spills out.

> IRIS
>
> I love buying wedding gifts!

Paula picks up the hairbrush and hands it to Iris.

> PAULA
>
> You like the color purple?

> IRIS
>
> I thought Oprah deserved an Oscar.

Paula translates, shakes it off.

> IRIS
>
> I mean, how often do you get a chance
> to give a gift that can change a life?

Paula hugs her.

PAULA
You are such a good friend.

Paula pulls out a map of the mall.

PAULA
First of all I think we should try and
locate James and Frank.

Iris brightens at this.

IRIS
Frank is here?

Paula nods.

PAULA
He's helping.

IRIS
I see.

Iris looks around. Paula spreads the map out and pulls out a pen. The map has various locations marked along with a trail to follow.

PAULA
I've charted a map of likely locations, based on where they shouldn't be, in ascending order of inappropriateness. Electronics hut. Sporting goods. Taco house. Beer garden. Video Game store.

Iris examines the intricate chart.

IRIS
I've always admired your Mall logistics.

PAULA
The key is Experience.

* * *

James and Frank are lost in The Twilight Zone.

The cashiers are all wearing dark suits and thin ties and smoking unfiltered cigarettes. The shoppers look like characters from the series:

The woman with the bandaged face.

William Shatner as the airline passenger.

The tall alien chef.

* * *

Elsewhere, Iris is happily shopping.

Paula drags her away to continue the hunt.

* * *

Frank points to something and writes it on the list.

James considers, then shakes his head.

Frank crosses it off the list.

*   *   *

A cacophony of TVs, each showing something different.

The noise is so loud that Paula and Iris can't hear each other. They are reduced to hand signals, like Navy Seals in enemy territory.

*   *   *

Frank points to something and writes it on the list.

James considers, then shakes his head.

Frank crosses it off the list.

*   *   *

Paula and Iris scan the Sporting Goods department with binoculars.

*   *   *

James and Frank hover at the edge of the China department.

James tries to drag Frank inside.

Frank resists

Vigorously.

The manager gives both a dirty look.

They exit quickly.

*   *   *

Paula and Iris wander by the Lingerie department.

Paula is intrigued by anything in red lace.

Iris drags Paula away to continue the hunt.

*   *   *

James and Frank are back at the fountain, sitting on the ledge.

They have no packages.

A vendor wagon is nearby. In swirling bright colors, the chalkboard sign says COFFEE.

> JAMES
> You want some coffee?

> FRANK
> Yeah.

James walks over to the vendor. There is no line.

> JAMES
> Two.

> VENDOR
> Two what?

James looks at the sign.

> JAMES
> Two coffees.

The Vendor shakes his head.

> VENDOR
> We don't have coffee.

James looks at the sign again.

> JAMES
> It says COFFEE.

The vendor shrugs.

> VENDOR
> It's a fluid market.

James looks at the sign once more.

> JAMES
> Coffee is a fluid.

> VENDOR
> Actually coffee is a suspension and an emulsion.

James considers this information.

It's not helpful.

James looks at the sign again.

> JAMES
> It says COFFEE.

> VENDOR
> It's a sign.

> JAMES
> What do you serve?

The vendor glances at his sign.

> VENDOR
> Espresso. Latte. Cappuccino.

James nods.

> JAMES
> Ah. And that won't.

> VENDOR
> Fit on the sign. Right.

> JAMES
> You could get a new sign.

> VENDOR
> But then I would miss these stimulating conversations.

James thinks.

> JAMES
> Coffee is stimulating.

> VENDOR
> So is Espresso. Latte. Cappuccino.

James thinks.

> JAMES
> Okay, give me two cappuccinos. Cappuccini?

James carries the two cups back to Frank.

They are very hot.

He hurries.

> JAMES
> Here.

He hands Frank a cup.

Frank opens the top and sees foam.

FRANK
What's this?

JAMES
Cappuccino. It's all they had.

FRANK
I wanted coffee.

James takes a sip.

It's VERY hot.

JAMES
It's all they had.

Frank points at the sign.

FRANK
It says COFFEE.

JAMES
It's a long story. Something about
fluids.

FRANK
Coffee is a fluid.

JAMES
Actually coffee is a suspension and an
emulsion.

Frank ponders this information.

FRANK
That's not helpful.

                    JAMES
    You're telling me.

Frank blows on the hot cappuccino.

The foam sprays all over James.

It is VERY hot.

                    FRANK
    Do you know how they make
    cappuccino?

James cleans himself off with a napkin.

                    JAMES
    Enlighten me.

James takes another sip. It's still VERY hot.

                    FRANK
    They put coffee beans and milk in this
    big barrel. And then elderly European
    women stomp all over it in their bare
    feet.

James and Frank gaze down into their cups.

They toss them away.

                    FRANK
    I really wanted coffee.

                    JAMES
    It's all they had.

Frank points to the sign.

                    FRANK
It says COFFEE.

                    JAMES
We live in suspension.

                    FRANK
Not to mention emulsion.

James goes back to the vendor.

                    JAMES
Give me an espresso and a cup of hot
water.

James pours the espresso into the water. He
walks back and offers the cup to Frank.

                    JAMES
Here.

                    FRANK
I knew it.

Frank points to the sign.

                    FRANK
It says COFFEE.

James nods.

                    JAMES
So what do we got?

Frank pulls out the list.

> FRANK
Number one is: a toaster.

> JAMES
What's number two?

Frank checks the list.

> FRANK
There is no number two.

James grabs the list.

> JAMES
That was our list an hour ago.

> FRANK
It's a compelling choice.

James takes a pen and crosses toaster off the list. A blender revs up at the vendor's wagon.

> JAMES
How about a blender?

Frank leaps up, almost spilling his suspended emulsion. James slides quickly out of range.

> FRANK
Are you nuts?

> JAMES
I'm here. With you. Shopping. What are the odds?

FRANK
Point taken.

JAMES
Anyway, what's wrong with a blender?

Frank shakes his head.

FRANK
Blenders are dangerous.

Frank takes a sip. It is VERY hot.

JAMES
How so?

Frank starts to blow on the cup in James' direction, then switches directions.

FRANK
More people are killed by blenders
than any other household device
except the television.

JAMES
How are people killed by a television?

FRANK
They turn it on.

Frank takes a sip. It's still hot.

James shakes his head.

JAMES
Where do you get these ideas?

Frank shrugs.

> FRANK
> Factuosity.com. These are true facts.

James sighs.

> JAMES
> What's a false fact?

Frank straightens James's tie.

> FRANK
> A false fact is, for example, I gave you a
> tie for each of the last three birthdays.

James examines his tie.

> JAMES
> You know, come to think of it, you did
> give me a tie for the last three
> birthdays. So how is that false?

> FRANK
> Because actually it was the last five
> birthdays.

> JAMES
> Point taken.

James stands.

> JAMES
> I think maybe we should split up. You
> re-enter the Twilight Zone. I'll see what
> I can hunt down in Jurassic Park.

Frank stands and throws away the rest of his COFFEE.

> FRANK
> Okay. Meet back here.

> JAMES
> It seems inevitable.

* * *

Paula and Iris enter and sit in the Food Court.

The sign on the coffee wagon has now changed to SNOW CONES.

> PAULA
> I don't know where they could be.

> IRIS
> We checked everywhere they
> shouldn't be.

Paula points to Jurassic Park.

> PAULA
> Have you ever noticed that nobody
> ever goes into that store?

Iris nods.

> IRIS
> I think they all use the tunnel.

They sit on the ledge of the fountain.

> IRIS
> So, what should we get the bride and
> groom?

> PAULA
> Not a toaster.

Iris sees the snow cone wagon.

> IRIS
> How about an ice crusher?

Paula slowly nods.

> PAULA
> That's very wise.

> IRIS
> What are friends for?

> PAULA
> Want a snow cone?

> IRIS
> Sure.

> PAULA
> What flavor?

Iris thinks for a moment.

> IRIS
> Coffee.

Paula goes to the Snow Cone stand.

Iris watches the shoppers.

Someone passes by with a new toaster.

She sighs.

Paula returns with two coffee-flavored snow cones.

> PAULA
> Tell you what. You wait here for them.
> I'll go looking where they should be:
> the china department, the crystal
> department, and the bridal registry.
> Wouldn't that be a shock?

> IRIS
> Completely.

> PAULA
> I'll meet you back here.

> IRIS
> Okay.

Paula takes a bite of her snow cone, then centers herself for the quest.

> PAULA
> To locate what's lost, you must first
> find yourself.

Iris frowns.

IRIS

You need to cut down on those Tai Chi lessons.

*   *   *

Frank wanders through the tunnel, having a serious bout of claustrophobia.

Other shoppers ignore him.

*   *   *

James meanders through the China department, afraid to touch anything.

The clerks take bets on how much he'll break.

*   *   *

In the Crystal department, Paula shows the clerks a picture of James.

They don't recognize him.

*   *   *

Frank is having Norwegian tacos (made with lefse) and flirting with the colorfully dressed waitress.

*   *   *

At the Bridal Registry, James is playing with the computer.

The printer starts printing.

It won't stop.

*   *   *

In the China department, Paula shows the clerks a picture of James.

They do recognize him, and all point in different directions.

*   *   *

Frank is having a pitcher of beer and flirting with the colorfully dressed waitress.

* * *

In the Silverware Department, James tries to guess the function of an oddly shaped pair of sterling silver tongs.

* * *

In the Bridal Registry, the printer is still printing.

No one can stop it.

Paula recognizes the hand of James.

* * *

At the Video Game store, Frank is playing Parsival II and flirting with the colorfully dressed salesclerk.

*   *   *

In the Furniture Department, James is exhausted and stops to lie on a couch and watch a ballgame.

*   *   *

In the Silverware Department, Paula pauses to arrange the silverware on the demo table so that the prongs on the forks line up evenly.

*   *   *

In the Women's Lingerie Department, James is slyly examining some red lingerie.

A saleswoman approaches him.

SALESWOMAN
Can I help you?

JAMES
No. Just. Passing through.

James tries to hide behind a rack.

                    SALESWOMAN
No need to be ashamed. Is this for you?

James slides farther behind the rack.

                    JAMES
No, it's not for me. Well, if I bought it,
it would be for me. I mean, my wife
would wear it but it would be for me.

                    SALESWOMAN
So it's for your wife?

                    JAMES
Yes. No.

The saleswoman moves close and nods
knowingly.

                    SALESWOMAN
Need to spice things up a bit?

                    JAMES
Not at all. We're spicy.

The saleswoman again nods knowingly.

                    SALESWOMAN
I understand.

James whispers back.

                    JAMES
Did she say something to you?

SALESWOMAN
Who?

JAMES
My wife. She shops here. Not here. But.
You know. Here.

The saleswoman shakes her head.

SALESWOMAN
I don't know your wife.

James nods, and accidentally backs into a mannequin dressed in red lace lingerie.

JAMES
Of course you don't. Otherwise, you'd
know that she has a full rack.

He struggles with the mannequin.

JAMES
Of spice I mean.

He tries to stand it back up. It falls again.

JAMES
Not that her uh–

He catches it, with his hands in awkward locations.

JAMES
I'm a very happy man.

He switches his hands.

                    JAMES
    Rack-wise.

The saleswoman does not approve.

                    SALESWOMAN
    Whatever you say.

He hands her the mannequin, then grabs a couple of other red items off the racks.

                    JAMES
    And one of these. And this too.

                    SALESWOMAN
    Whatever you say.

He hands her a credit card.

                    SALESWOMAN
    You know we also have some very
    attractive items in the Menswear
    department.

                    JAMES
    No thanks. I never. I mean.

The saleswoman nods.

                    SALESWOMAN
    I understand.

She hands him a big shopping bag.

                    JAMES
    Mum's the word.

The saleswoman nods.

SALESWOMAN
I'm sure it is.

James walks away, trying to hide his face behind the bag.

The saleswoman shakes her head.

SALESWOMAN
Another unsatisfied customer.

*   *   *

Iris is waiting at the fountain, eating a snow cone. Frank approaches, carrying a package.

FRANK
Hey!

IRIS
Hi!

They both say:

BOTH
Have you seen—

Then laugh.

IRIS
What's in the package?

>   FRANK
> Wedding gift for James and Paula.

Iris sits on the fountain ledge.

>   IRIS
> You're about ten years late.

Frank sits next to her.

>   FRANK
> They're giving it to our Cousin Angela.

>   IRIS
> Ah. What are you giving her?

>   FRANK
> Nothing. We don't have a Cousin
> Angela.

>   IRIS
> Then she'll probably like whatever you
> don't give her.

Frank stares intently at Iris.

>   FRANK
> That's very wise.

>   IRIS
> So what's in the package?

Frank holds it up proudly.

>   FRANK
> A toaster.

> IRIS
Really?

Iris puts out her hand to touch it gently.

> FRANK
Highest wattage.

> IRIS
Really?

Both hands.

> FRANK
Gets very hot.

> IRIS
To the touch.

They move closer, peer at one another directly over the box.

> FRANK
You could get burned.

> IRIS
Because it's hot.

They stand up together, lost in each other's eyes, hands caressing the toaster.

Iris turns away.

> IRIS
I haven't had toast since my divorce.

FRANK
That's a long time without toast.

IRIS
A long. Long. Time.

FRANK
You could try my toaster?

She turns back, wary.

IRIS
How do you like your bagels?

FRANK
Cream cheese.

IRIS
Oh my.

FRANK
You know what I like about bagels?

IRIS
What?

Her breathing is fast and shallow.

FRANK
No crumbs.

Iris grabs Frank's hand and they rush off.

*　　*　　*

Paula comes into the food court and looks around for Iris.

She walks over to the vendor wagon.

                    PAULA
    I'd like a snow cone.

The vendor shakes his head.

                    VENDOR
    No snow cones.

                    PAULA
    What are you selling?

                    VENDOR
    Toast.

                    PAULA
    Good luck with that.

Paula returns to the fountain and waits. James comes in carrying a shopping bag.

                    JAMES
    What are you doing here?

                    PAULA
    I thought maybe you could use some
    help shopping. But you seem to be
    doing fine. What did you get?

James tries to hide the shopping bag.

                    JAMES
Nothing.

Paula looks around him.

                    PAULA
You bought something.

                    JAMES
Yes. No.

She reaches around him for the bag.

                    PAULA
Show me.

                    JAMES
Tools.

Paula is unconvinced.

                    PAULA
You're giving tools as a wedding gift?

                    JAMES
No. Yes.

She shrugs.

                    PAULA
Well, she's your cousin.

James shrugs.

                    JAMES
No. Yes.

Paula reaches for the bag again.

>   PAULA
> What kind of tools?

>   JAMES
> Uh.

Paula grabs the bag.

>   PAULA
> Let me see.

>   JAMES
> It's not exactly–

She looks in the bag.

>   JAMES
> Tools in the, uh, normal sense.

Paula looks at James.

>   PAULA
> This is lingerie.

>   JAMES
> So it seems.

She holds up a red lace bra.

>   PAULA
> Just how well do you know Cousin
> Angela?

>   JAMES
> Never met her.

Then matching panties.

> PAULA
> Are you having an affair?

> JAMES
> No.

She puts her hand on his shoulder.

> PAULA
> Are you...do you like...

> JAMES
> No! Not on me anyway.

She puts the bag down.

> PAULA
> Then I don't understand. Why did you buy these?

> JAMES
> You had to be there.

She sits on the ledge of the fountain.

> PAULA
> Are you not happy with...

> JAMES
> No! I mean. Yes! I mean. Wait.

He kneels down beside her.

> PAULA
> We're not newlyweds anymore.

JAMES
We never were!

PAULA
What does that mean?

JAMES
Something other than the way it
sounded.

The conversation is getting louder. People are
starting to notice.

PAULA
Don't I excite you anymore?

JAMES
Of course. Absolutely. I was just talking
about your rack.

Paula stands.

PAULA
My what?

He stands too.

JAMES
The sales lady asked. And I told her
your rack was full. Spicy!

A crowd starts to gather.

PAULA
You told who what?

                    JAMES
     At the time. I meant it as. In the
     situation.

He hands her the bag.

                    JAMES
     Here. I bought these. As a gift. For you.
     Well. For me. But. You would wear
     them.

Paula pulls the lingerie out of the bag. She
holds each article up so everyone can see.

James tries to block the view.

Unsuccessfully.

                    PAULA
     Is this what you want?

James looks around for help.

None comes.

                    JAMES
     Not only do I have no idea what the
     right answer is, I have no idea if there
     is a right answer.

Paula nods.

                    PAULA
     Fine.

Paula takes off her blouse.

James desperately revolves between trying to talk to her and trying to shield her from view.

Paula takes off her jeans.

James is unsuccessful.

> JAMES
> What–

Paula takes off her white lace bra.

> JAMES
> What–

And puts on the sexy red one.

> JAMES
> Are you–

Paula slips out of her white lace panties.

James holds up the huge shopping bag to cover her.

> JAMES
> Everyone can–

Paula slips into the new red lace panties.

Now a BIG crowd has gathered.

Paula slides into the red lace teddy and jumps up on the ledge of the fountain.

There is loud applause from the men in the crowd.

Paula struts around the circular fountain ledge. The crowd, now a mob, flows around the fountain to follow her.

Tourists take pictures.

Paula leaps into the fountain and begins splashing around, getting soaked.

Mall security personnel congregate, forming an action plan. In the noise, they are reduced to hand signals, like Navy Seals in enemy territory.

PAULA

Are you happy now?

The crowd cheers.

James looks around, then jumps into the fountain with her.

JAMES

Yes. Yes. I'm happy.

PAULA

You are?

JAMES

I didn't buy these for you because this
is who I want you to be. I bought these
for you because this is who you are.
Obviously.

Paula is confused.

JAMES

That's what love is: eternal
unblinkableness. This is how I see you.
How I have always seen you. How I
will always see you.

PAULA

You do?

JAMES

Yes. You are fearless. You are
dauntless. You are... the wildest woman
I have ever known.

James looks around at the crowd.

JAMES

Obviously.

PAULA

I am?

JAMES

I love that about you. I always have.
The Wild You.

James climbs up on the ledge of the fountain
with Paula.

JAMES

This is my wife!

The crowd cheers once more.

PAULA
I never—

He leaps back into the fountain, takes her in his arms, kisses her.

The crowd applauds wildly.

PAULA
I didn't think you remembered.

JAMES
I'm a man. There are many things I could and will forget. This is not one of them. You are not one of them.

She kisses him this time.

JAMES
Do you want to go home?

PAULA
I do.

Security officers are now climbing into the fountain.

She holds them off with a finger.

Not that one.

JAMES
Do you want to change?

PAULA
Should I?

James shakes his head.

PAULA

Never.

PAULA

Then let's go.

She leaps out of the fountain onto the ledge, then gracefully steps down and away, leaving a glittering trail for James to follow.

The crowd parts for her.

The security officers just watch.

James also watches for a minute. Then he rushes after her.

The Lingerie Saleswoman whispers in the Vendor's ear. He changes his sign to say in bright swirling colors: LINGERIE.

The crowd surrounds them.

THE RETURN

In 1961, a group of social anthropologists, eminent in their field and expert in all human cultures, gathered to ascertain the secret to a good marriage. Their report is expected any day now.

www.Factuosity.com

In their apartment, Paula and James are ready to go. S.C.U.B.A. dreams quietly on the loveseat.

PAULA

Got the gift?

James picks it up. It's about the size of a toaster.

JAMES

Right here.

As they open the door, the Bartletts across the hall are also leaving, also dressed up, also with a gift.

PAULA

Hi.

> MRS. BARTLETT

Hello.

James and Mr. Bartlett exchange wary nods.

> PAULA

Where are you off to?

> MRS. BARTLETT

Our Cousin Angela is getting married.

James drops the gift.

> MRS. BARTLETT

Where are you off to?

James picks up the gift.

> JAMES

Mall of America.

Mrs. Bartlett points to the gift in James hands.

> MRS. BARTLETT

Are you returning that?

Paula turns to James.

They both look at the gift and break into laughter.

The Bartletts are very confused.

James hands the gift to Mrs. Bartlett.

JAMES

Please give this to your cousin with our
best wishes.

MRS. BARTLETT

No. Really. We couldn't.

PAULA

We insist.

MRS. BARTLETT

You don't even know her.

JAMES

We feel like she's one of the family.

Mrs. Bartlett accepts it with a curious look.

MRS. BARTLETT

That's very nice of you. Thank you.

She nods and passes the gift to Mr. Bartlett,
who looks at it with deep suspicion.

MRS. BARTLETT

We better go.

James nods.

JAMES

Don't want to be late for Cousin
Angela!

Paula laughs.

> PAULA

Bye!

The Bartletts leave.

James calls out to them.

> JAMES

After you.

Paula waves then turns to James.

> PAULA

You never told me. What did you finally get?

> JAMES

An ice crusher.

Paula nods.

> PAULA

That's very wise.

She kisses his cheek.

He puts his arms around her.

> JAMES

The card said: *I have no idea who you are, but I wish you all of the happiness that we have had.*

> PAULA

Also very wise.

James smiles.

JAMES
I have a gift for you.

He hands her a small box. She opens it.

PAULA
Diamonds?

JAMES
Better. Dodecahedral zirconium.

PAULA
I love it!

JAMES
I have another gift for you.

James drops his pants and models his red silk boxers.

PAULA
So you're telling me that the secret to a good marriage is red underwear.

James ponders this for a moment.

JAMES
I'm not telling you. I'm showing you.

She unbuttons her blouse, showing the red lingerie underneath, and struts back into the apartment.

James waddles after her and shuts the door.

The hallway is silent but for the muffled barking of a spaniel-husky mix.

EPILOGUE

"Do you think you will get married again," Iris asked.

Frank paused then said:

"One day, many people will have asked me what I thought of marriage, and at that time I will say as I will have said many times in the future past, that marriage is a fine institution to which everyone should have been committed at least once."

Iris nodded.

"Do you think you will get married again?" Frank asked.

The bagel popped up, golden. She handed him half and reached for the cream cheese.

"My father used to tell a story about a man from Duluth. Or was it Brainerd? Maybe it was Red Wing. Anyway every morning this man would get up and first thing he would hit himself in the head with a two-by-four. 'Why do you hit yourself in the head with a two-by-four?' people asked him. And he answered: 'Why ruin a good piece of iron?' "

Frank nodded.

"Pass the cream cheese, honey."

ABOUT THE AUTHOR

Stephen Evans is a playwright and the author of *The Island of Always, Painting Sunsets,* and *Funny Thing Is: A Guide to understanding Comedy.*

Find him online at:

https://www.istephenevans.com/

https://www.facebook.com/iStephenEvans

https://twitter.com/iStephenEvans

Books by Stephen Evans

Fiction:

The Marriage of True Minds

Let Me Count the Ways

The Island of Always

Two Short Novels

Painting Sunsets

The Mind of a Writer and other Fables

Non-Fiction:

A Transcendental Journey

Funny Thing Is: A Guide to Understanding Comedy

The Laughing String: Thoughts on Writing

Layers of Light

Liebestraum

Plays:

The Ghost Writer

Spooky Action at a Distance

Tourists

Generations (with Morey Norkin and Michael Gilles)

The Visitation Quartet

As You Like It (Adaptation)

Verse:

Sonets from the Chesapeke

A Look from Winter

Limerosity

Limerositus